CHAMPAK

Test Your Memory

Published in Moonstone
by Rupa Publications India Pvt. Ltd 2024
7/16, Ansari Road, Daryaganj
New Delhi 110002

Sales Centres:
Bengaluru Chennai
Hyderabad Jaipur Kathmandu
Kolkata Mumbai Prayagraj

Copyright © Delhi Press Patra Prakashan Pvt. Ltd., 2024

All rights reserved.
No part of this publication may be reproduced, transmitted, or stored in a retrieval system, in any form or by any means, electronic, mechanical, photocopying, recording or otherwise, without the prior permission of the publisher.

P-ISBN: 978-93-6156-503-8
E-ISBN: 978-93-6156-978-4

First impression 2024

10 9 8 7 6 5 4 3 2 1

Printed in India
This book is sold subject to the condition that it shall not, by way of trade or otherwise, be lent, resold, hired out, or otherwise circulated, without the publisher's prior consent, in any form of binding or cover other than that in which it is published.

Look at the picture and answer the following questions:

Q1. How many children are covered under blankets?

Q2.How many round snow shapes can you see?

Q3. How many snow games can you spot?

January 26 is Republic Day. Look at the picture and answer the following questions:

Q1. How many flags can you count?

Q2.What float have the Champakvan animals made?

Q3. Where does the republic day parade take place?

Clean the Clutter

Q1. What are the kids doing?
Q2.In which bin will you throw a broken computer?
Q3. What item is being reused?
Q4. How many bins are there?

June 30 is Asteroid Day. An asteroid is a chunk of rock and metal in outer space that is in orbit around the Sun. An asteroid belt contains many soild, odd-shaped asteroids.Look at the picture and answer the following questions:

Q1. Where is the asteroid belt located?

Q2.How many planets can you count?

Q3. Which planet is the closest to the sun?

On July 22, 2019, Chandrayaan 2, India's second mission to the Moon, was launched from Satish Dhawan Space Centre, Sriharikota. Moons are of many colours. Look at the picture and answer the following questions:

Q1. How many moons did you count?

Q2. Which colours do you see?

Q3. Which of these moons have you seen in the sky?

Simran has gone for a walk at the Lodhi Gardens with her father. Observe the picture below and then answer the questions.

Q1. How many people are walking on the track?

Q2. What is the colour of thedog-walker's shirt?

Q3. What are the two girls doing in front of the tomb?

Q4. How many benches are there near the flowers?

Observe the picture for a whole minute. Then cover it and try answering the following questions:

Q1. How many toy ships can you count?
Q2. What is the colour of the towel?
Q3. What is the shape of the soap?
Q4. What is the colour of the cat's tail?

Wetland Swim

February 2 is World Wetlands Day. A wetland is a place where the land is covered with water permanently or seasonally. For example, marshes. ponds, edge Look at the image below and answer the following questions:

Q1. What is the human-made wetland called?

Q2. In which wetland are turtles found? Q3. How many alligators can you count?

Q4. Name one migratory bird.

World Hippo Day is on February 15. Look at the picture and answer the following questions:

Q1. How many hippos can you count in total? Q2. How many hippos are in the water? Q3. How many teeth are easily visible when hippos open their mouth?

Q4. What do you think the hippos with open mouths are doing?

Women of Steel

International Women's Day. Look at the picture below and answer the following questions:

Q1. Name the famous woman who fought for education.

Q2. Identify the sports icons.

Q3. What global issue are the students fighting for?

Q4. Identify the first Indian woman to go into space.

This year, we celebrate Holi on March 29. Observe the picture and answer the following questions:

Q1. Which holi colours are placed on the table?

Q2. What colour pichkari the girl in the yellow skirt is holding?

Q3. Identify the snacks. Q4. How many kids are playing Holi?

It is International Children's Book Day on April 2. Look at the picture and answer the following questions:

Q1. How many children are reading books?

Q2. Where do you think they are reading them? Q3. What is the girl at the bottom holding in her hand? Q4. Name one fiction book.

June 8 is World Ocean Day. Look at the picture and answer the following questions:

Q1. Identify an odd object in the picture that should not be found underwater.

Q2. How many different creatures can you see? Q3. What do you call a group of fish swimming in the same direction?

Q4. How many fish have stripes on their bodies?

Look at the picture and answer the following questions:

Q1. How many animals can you spot in the picture?

Q2. Which animals are in the water?

Q3. Name the animals that have horns.

Q4. How many wild boars can you see in the picture?

National Education Day in India is celebrated on November 11. Look at the picture and answer the following questions:

Q1. How many books can you count in the picture?

Q2. Name the items on the teacher's desk. Q3. Which colour book is the boy in the front holding? Q4. Do you prefer indoor or outdoor classrooms?

November 21 is World Television Day. Look at the picture and answer the following questions:

Q1. How many television sets do you see in the picture below?

Q2. Which television has the most number of buttons?

Q3. How many televisions have antennae?

Look at the picture below and answer the following questions:

Q1. How many students are studying science?

Q2. For which subject are the students using a globe?

Q3. Whose photograph are the students looking at in the history study group?

Q4. Name your favourite subject.

Look at the picture and answer the following questions:

Q1. How many dancers can you count?

Q2. Which international dance forms can you identify?

Q3. Which Indian dance forms can you identify?

Q4. In which dance form does the dancer wear a hat?

Look at the picture and answer the questions.

Q1. How many kids are kayaking?

Q2. In which activity are kids using ropes?

Q3. Which two activities begin with the letter 'P'?

Q4. What is your favourite activity in summer camps?

World Milk Day is observed on June 1. Look at the picture and answer th questions:
Q1. How many animals can you count?
Q2.At the milk farm, what is collected and disctributed? Q3. How many pails is the man on the cycle carrying?
Q4. How many pails can you count in total?

Vyshana and Sahil made one rakhi each. Look at the picture below and answer the following questions:

Q1. Name the festival Rakhi is tied to?

Q2. Identify the common colour in Vyshana and Sahil's rakhi. Q3. How many triangular beads can you count? Q4. Whose rakhi has a blue stone?

World First Aid Day is on September 14. Look at the picture and answer the following questions:

Q1. What item can you see inside the first-aid box?

Q2. Which machine takes pictures of bones?

Q3. Name any 3 items kept outside the first aid box. Q4.What is the doctor carrying in his pocket?

Social Distance

The French Open tennis event is ongoing amid the coronavirus pandemic. Several safety rules have been enforced in the game. Look at the picture and answer the following questions:

Q1. What is different about this tennis match? Q2. Does the trophy belong to this tennis event? Q3. Why are the seats vacant?

Q4. How many sanitizer dispensers can you see?

It's World Tsunami Awareness Day on November 5. Tsunamis are giant, powerful waves most often caused by earthquakes beneath the ocean floor. Look at the picture and answer the following questions :

Q1. How many sirens are running?

Q2. Where is the evacuation zone?

Q3. How many people are running in the wrong direction?

India at Sea

December 4 is National Navy Day in India. Look at the picture and answer the following questions:

Q1. How many flags can you count?

Q2. Where is the aeroplane landing?

Q3. What colour is the Indian Navy uniform?

Q4. Do you see a submarine?

Seasonal Sleepers

What is hibernation?

Hibernation is a way that some animals deal with the harshness of winter. They curl up in a safe place and stay there until the winter ends. Hibernating animals prepare for winter with extra eating. They store fat to keep them alive during the months. In warmer weather, they return to their regular activities and slow down their bodies to save energy.

Look at the picture and answer the questions.

Q1. Identify the hibernating animals.

Q2. Where is the snail hibernating?

Q3. Which of these animals are reptiles?

Q4. Which two animals hibernate in caves?

Indian Army Day is celebrated on January 15 in recognition of Field Marshal Kodandera M. Cariappa, the first Commander-in-Chief of the Indian Army.
Observe the picture and answer the questions.

Q1. Which day is being celebrated?

Q2. What is the name of the memorial in front of which soldiers are marching?

Q3. In which city is Amar Jawan Jyoti located?

Observe this scene from a literature festival and answer the questions.

Q1. How many people are on the panel?

Q2. What is written on the board behind the panel?

Q3. What is the girl standing in front of the stage holding in her hand?

Q4. What is the boy in the red cap doing?

Basant Panchami is being celebrated on February 10. Observe the picture and answer the questions below.

Q1. How many people are playing the dhol?

Q2. How many people are dancing?

Q3. What is the colour of the women's bangles? Q4. Name the different colours on the girl's kite. Q5. What is laid out on the table?

World Heritage Day is celebrated on April 18. A class has come to visit the group of monuments at Mahabalipuram, one of the world heritage sites in Tamil Nadu. Observe the picture and answer the questions given below.

Q1. What is the name of the monument?

Q2. What are the two students sitting on the rocks doing?

Q3. How many students are standing along with their teacher?

It's play day at the park. Observe the picture and answer the questions.

Q1. What is the colour of the boy's t-shirt who is blindfolded?

Q2.How many kids are on the slide?

Q3. What is the girl in front of the slide doing?

Q4. What is the boy behind the bush doing?

Observe the picture and answer the following questions:

Q1. What is the colour of the umbrella the boy sitting in front is holding?

Q2.What are the two kids putting on the girl's hair sitting in front of them?

Q3. What are the two girls sitting on the third row eating?

Father's Day is celebrated on June 16. Observe the picture and answer the questions.

Q1. What is written on the greeting card placed beside the cake?

Q2. How many candles are placed on the cake?

Q3. How many waiters are serving food to the couple?

Q4. What is the boy holding in his hand?

World UFO Day is celebrated on July 2. On this day, people gather together and watch the skies for unidentified flying objects (UFOs). Observe the picture and answer the questions. Q1. How many kids are standing with the man who is looking through the telescope? Q2. What is the lady standing beside the dog using to watch the sky?

Q3. How many kids are enjoying a picnic on the mat?

Q4. Is there a cat on the terrace?

Guru Purnima is celebrated on July 21. Observe the picture and answer the questions.

Q1. Which instrument is the teacher playing?

Q2. How many kids are surrounding the teacher?

Q3. What is the girl in a purple dress holding in her hands?

Q4. How many flowers is the boy holding?

This year, Raksha Bandhan is being celebrated on August 19. Observe the picture and answer the following questions:

Q1. How many rakhis can you count?

Q2. Which sweets can you see in the picture?

Q3. What are the two girls doing?

Q4. What is the boy hiding behind his back?

Ganesh Chaturthi is celebrated on September 7. Observe the picture and answer the following questions:

Q1. Which musical instruments can you find in the picture?

Q2. Name the white sweet.

October 4 is World Animal Welfare Day. Observe the picture and answer the questions.

Q1. What is the girl feeding the dog?

Q2. How many cats can you count?

Q3. What is written on the shirts worn by the animals?

Food from several countries is being distributed to children in orphanages. Look at the picture below and answer the following questions:

Q1. What slogans can you see?

Q2. How many countries can you count?

Q3. Name three foreign food dishes.

World Fisheries Day is celebrated on November 21. This day highlights the importance of healthy oceans and seas—home to the fishes. Look at the image below and answer the following questions:

Q1. How many fisherwomen are carrying baskets?

Q2. How many birds can you count at the bay?

Q3. How many boats are anchored?

Super-Abled

International Day of Persons with Disabilities is celebrated on December 3. Look at the picture and answer the questions.

Q1. How many sports are being played?

Q2. How many athletes are participating in the games?

Q3.What is the referee holding by the swimming pool holding his hand?

Observe the picture for a minute, cover it and try answering the questions given below.

Q1. What does the circular signboard say?

Q2. How many children are waiting with their parents?

Q3. How many buses are there on the road?

Q4. Is the dog running ahead on the leash? Q5. What is the name of the tea stall?

Observe the picture, cover it and try answering the questions below.
Q1. What is the colour of the toy car? Q2. Who is eating the ice cream?
Q3. What fruits are growing on the tree? Q4. How many ducks are in the pond? Q5. What is the boy in the blue shorts doing?

Observe the picture for a minute, cover it and try answering the questions given below:

Q1. How many pots of money plants are hanging?

Q2. What is the colour of the seed packets?

Q3. How are the plants getting water? Q4. What sapling is the little girl planting?

Q5. What is written on the board?

May 7 is Rabindranath Tagore Jayanti. Observe the picture of Santiniketan given below for one minute, cover the page and answer the questions.

Q1. What poem are the children learning?

Q2. What is the tourist taking a photo of? Q3. What is the colour of the children's uniform? Q4. How many birds are sitting on the banyan tree?

Q5. In which year was Rabindra Bhavan established?

Observe the picture given below for a minute, cover the page and answer the questions given below.

Q1. How many bowls of kheer is the girl carrying?

Q2. What is the boy in the orange kurta doing?

Q3. What are the dishes being served? Q4. How many people are sitting on the left table? Q5. What is the colour of the table cloth?

July 11 is World Population Day. Observe the picture for a minute, cover it and try answering the questions given in the box.

Q1. Which countries have negative population growth?

Q2. What is written on the chart paper? Q3. Who is making a presentation in front of the classroom? Q4. How many students are present in the class?

Q5. What is the teacher doing?

On August 15, 2018 India celebrates its Independence Day. Observe the picture for a minute, cover the page and answer the questions given below.

Q1. What is the boy in the white cap doing?

Q2. What is the colour of the students' uniform?

Q3. Name 2 freedom fighters whose photos are on the stage?

Q4. How many people are saluting the flag?

Einsteins-in-Making

On the occasion of International Literacy Day, a science exhibition is held in the classroom. Observe the picture for a minute, cover the page and answer the questions given below.

Q1. How many visitors have come along with the principal? Q2. What is the colour of the school uniform? Q3. What is the project being presented by the girl? Q4. What is written on the blackboard? Q5. What is the colour of the windmill?

World Heart Day is celebrated on September 29. Observe the picture given below, cover the page and answer the following questions:

Q1. What food are the kids sitting on the bench, eating?

Q2. Who is running on the walking track?

Q3. How many women are there among the senior citizens who are exercising?

Q4. What is the colour of the slide in the park?

On the occasion of Navratri, there is a celebration happening. Cover the picture and answer the questions:

Q1. How many kids are playing garba?

Q2. How many singers are singing on stage? Q3. What is the shape of the Rangoli?

Q4. What are the delicacies in the sweet shop?

World Food Day is celebrated on October 16. There's a food festival happening at the school. Observe the picture given below, cover the picture and answer the questions.

Q1. What is the girl standing in front of the American food stall eating?

Q2. What is the chef from the Chinese food stall serving his customer?

Q3. How many food stalls are laid out?

Children's Day!

Observe the picture for a minute, cover it and try answering the questions.
Q1. How many teachers are performing on stage? Q2. What is the colour of their uniform? Q3. How many students are sitting in the front row?
Q4. What is written on the banner placed on top of the stage?

All India Handicrafts Week is celebrated from December 8 to December 14. Observe the picture, cover the page and answer the questions.

Q1. How many stalls are there in the exhibition? Q2. What is the colour of the Bandhini print at the Bandhini stall? Q3. How many kids have come to the exhibition?

Q4. What is the woman selling at the Madhubani stall?

On The Bus!

Observe this picture for one minute and try answering the questions without looking at the picture.

Q1. Where is the bus headed? Q2. What colour was the children's school uniform? Q3. What was the man carrying in the basket? Q4. What was the pickpocket stealing? Q5. How many passengers were not seated?

Career Day

Observe the picture for a minute, cover it and try answering the questions below:
Q1. How many posters were put up on the board? Q2. What was the date on the board? Q3. What colour was the rock sample?
Q4. How many kids were taking notes?
Q5. What was the design on the vase?

Footpath Frolic

Observe the picture for a minute, cover it and try answering the questions given in the box.

Q1. How many were drinking tender coconut water?

Q2. What was the announcement on the poster about?

Q3. Describe the photo in the newspaper. Q4. What was the little girl holding?

Q5. What colour was the man's turban?

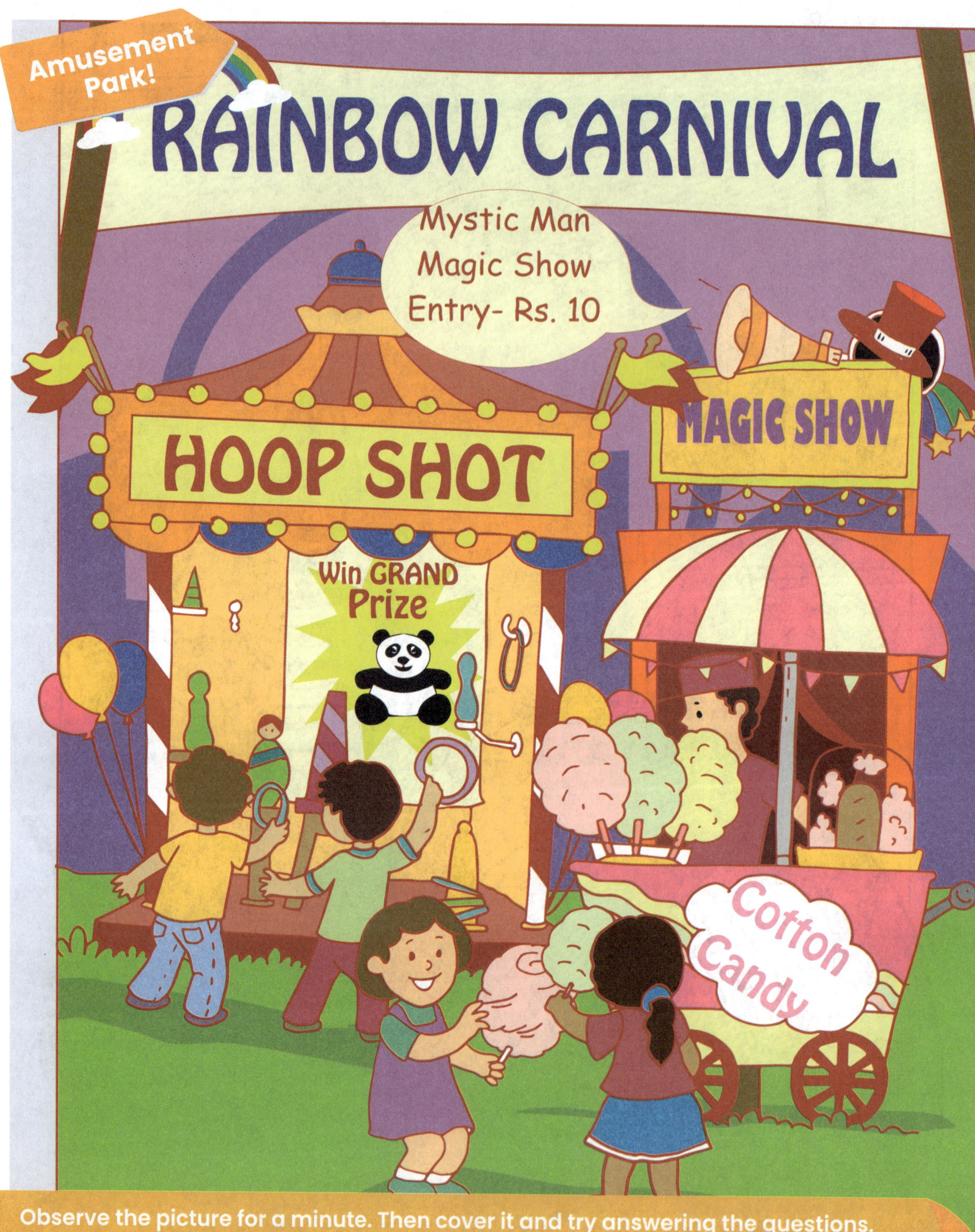

Observe the picture for a minute. Then cover it and try answering the questions.

Q1. How many different colours of cotton candy were being sold?

Q2. What was the grand prize for the hoop game?

Q3. What was the carnival's name?

Q4. What was the cost of the ticket to the magic show?

Observe this picture for one minute and try answering the questions without looking at the picture.

Q1. How many colours of balloons were there? Q2. What book was the father reading? Q3. How many candles were there on the cake?

Q4. What did the dog have in its mouth?

Q5. What was written on the balloon?

Observe the picture for a minute, cover it and try answering the questions below:
Q1. How many birds are in the picture? Q2. What fruits are growing on the trees?
Q3. What were the squirrels doing? Q4. What colours are the butterfly's wings?
Q5. What is the girl collecting in her book?

September 29 is World Maritime Day. Observe the picture of this bay for a minute, cover it and try answering the questions given in the box.

Q1. How many red boats are in the picture?

Q2. How many otters are swimming on their backs?

Q3. Is the sea lion sitting alone on the rock looking at the jetty or the sea?

Q4. What is written on the board?

It's penalty kick time! Look at this picture for two minutes. Then cover the picture and answer the questions given below:

Q1. How many girls are playing football?

Q2. What colour is the goalkeeper's jersey? Q3. What is the jersey number of the kicker? Q4. What time is it? Q5. Is it raining in the picture?

Observe the image for a minute and then answer the questions given below:
Q1. Which movie are the children watching?
Q2. How many boys are in the classroom?
Q3. What are the two girls in the back doing? Q4. What is the colour of the curtains? Q5. Which standard are the kids studying in?

Observe the picture for a minute, cover it and try answering the questions given below:

Q1. How much time is left for the New Year?

Q2. How many children are wearing party hats? Q3. What instruments are the musicians playing? Q4. What's the dress code for the men at the party?

Look at the picture of a bakery for a minute. Cover the picture and try answering the questions below:

Q1: What was the woman buying? Q2: What was the little girl eating?

Q3: What was the picture on the apron? Q4: How many donuts were left?

Q5: What was the amount on the billing machine?

Look at the picture of a park for a minute. Cover the picture and try answering the questions given below:

Q1: On which squares was the girl standing? Q2: How many girls were there in the park? Q3: What fruit was on the tree?

Q4: Which game were the two boys playing?

Q5: What was the colour of the dog's collar?

Look at the picture of a farm for a minute. Cover the picture and try answering the questions:

Q1: What vegetables were in the kids' baskets?

Q2: Among the animals, there was one that did not belong to the farm. Which one was it? Q3: What colour was the scarecrow's dress?

Q4: How many cows were there?

Look at the picture of a kitchen for a minute. Cover the picture and try answering the questions below:

Q1: How many apples were there? Q2: What was the design on the chef's apron?

Q3: What fridge magnets were there?

Q4: How many mice were there? Q5: What flavour of jam was on the fridge?

Observe this picture of kids making lamps for Diwali for one minute and try answering the following questions:

Q1. How many lamps were lit?

Q2. What shape was the boy cutting the clay in?

Q3. What colour was the girl painting the lamp?

Q4. What was written on the girl's t-shirt? Q5. Name the plant on the terrace.

Observe this picture for one minute. Cover it and then try answering the questions below:

Q1. How many people were on stage?

Q2. How many were playing string instruments?

Q3. What was the colour of the singer's sari?

Q4. How many focus lights were there?